**Dear Parents and Teachers,**

In an easy-reader format, **My Readers** introduce classic stories to children who are learning to read. Although favorite characters and time-tested tales are the basis for **My Readers**, the books tell completely new stories and are freshly and beautifully illustrated.

My Readers are available in three levels:

 Level One is for the emergent reader and features repetitive language and word clues in the illustrations.

Level Two is for more advanced readers who still need support saying and understanding some words. Stories are longer with word clues in the illustrations.

Level Three is for independent, fluent readers who enjoy working out occasional unfamiliar words. The stories are longer and divided into chapters.

Encourage children to select books based on interests, not reading levels. Read aloud with children, showing them how to use the illustrations for clues. With adult guidance and rereading, children will eventually read the desired book on their own.

Here are some ways you might want to use this book with children:

- Talk about the title and the cover illustrations. Encourage the child to use these to predict what the story is about.
- Discuss the interior illustrations and try to piece together a story based on the pictures. Does the child want to change or adjust his first prediction?
- After children reread a story, suggest they retell or act out a favorite part.

My Readers will not only help children become readers, they will serve as an introduction to some of the finest classic children's books available today.

—LAURA ROBB
Educator and Reading Consultant

For activities and reading tips, visit myreadersonline.com.

To Bixby and Van

—M. H.

SQUARE
FISH

An Imprint of Macmillan Children's Publishing Group

Printed in China by Toppan Leefung, Dongguan City, Guangdong Province.
For information, address Square Fish, 175 Fifth Avenue, New York, NY 10010.

Library of Congress Cataloging-in-Publication Data
Barbo, Maria S.
The Velveteen Rabbit and the boy / story by Maria Barbo ;
illustrated by Michael Hague ; inspired by Margery Williams's The Velveteen Rabbit. — 1st ed.
p. cm. — (My readers. Level 1)
Summary: The boy and rabbit from the classic story "The Velveteen Rabbit"
go for a walk in the woods and play games.
[1. Rabbits—Fiction. 2. Friendship—Fiction. 3. Play—Fiction.]
I. Hague, Michael, ill. II. Bianco, Margery Williams, 1881–1944. Velveteen rabbit. III. Title.
PZ7.B233443Ve 2012 [E]—dc22 2011009834

ISBN 978-0-312-60269-7 (hardcover)
1 3 5 7 9 10 8 6 4 2

ISBN 978-0-312-60366-3 (paperback)
1 3 5 7 9 10 8 6 4 2

Book design by Patrick Collins/Véronique Lefèvre Sweet

Square Fish logo designed by Filomena Tuosto

First Edition: 2012

myreadersonline.com
mackids.com

This is a Level 1 book

LEXILE: AD60L

The Velveteen Rabbit and the Boy

Maria S. Barbo illustrated by **Michael Hague**

inspired by
Margery Williams's *The Velveteen Rabbit*

SQUARE
FISH

Macmillan Children's Publishing Group
New York

Rabbit loved the Boy.

The Boy loved Rabbit.

The Boy ran to the woods.
Rabbit ran, too.

The Boy hopped like a bunny.

Rabbit hopped, too.

The Boy sang a song.

Rabbit sang, too.

"Hippy hop. Hippy hay.
What a great day to play!"

They played hide-and-seek.

Where did the Boy go?

"Here I am!"

Swoop.

The Boy gave Rabbit a big hug.

"Let's play pirates!"
said the Boy.

The Boy liked this game.

Rabbit liked it, too.

They made a ship.

They put up a flag.

"I will look for gold,"
said the Boy.

Was the gold
under the rock?

No.

Was the gold behind the tree?

No.

Where did the Boy go?

The sky grew dark.

The wind blew.

A raindrop hit Rabbit's nose.

A storm was coming!

Rabbit heard a big crash.

Was it thunder?

No!

It was the Boy!

Swoop!

The Boy gave Rabbit
a big hug.

"Let's race home!"
said the Boy.
They sang as they ran.

"Hippy hop. Hippy hay.
What a great day to play!"

Rabbit loved his Boy.

And the Boy loved Rabbit.